Handsome Boy

You Should Smile More

Written By
Mother-Son Duo
Eboni and Tristen Carroll

Illustrated By
Sameer Kassar

Tristen.

First paperback edition February 2021
ISBN: 978-0-578-83384-2

Library of Congress Catalog Number: 2021900571
Printed in the United States of America

Published by Little Eboni Einsteins Publications LLC
Duluth, GA
www.littleebonieinsteins.com

DEDICATION

To all the handsome boys,
With skin of darker hue,
No matter what this world seems to think of you,
They won't always know royalty when it arrives.
There's power in your skin and magic in your smile.

Smile anyway, it'll take their breath away

"Mommy, mommy, look!" Trent screams.
"Another tooth loose, let's see what the tooth fairy brings."

Now, take it easy, let's see what the dentist says.

"Can we hurry and get dressed?"
"Let's not be late," he begs.

Trent waits and waits, hoping to hear his name called soon.
"I wonder if she will leave more than a dollar.
Maybe this time she'll leave two."

Try not to think about it too much,
Focus on all the great things in store.
Handsome boy, you should smile more.

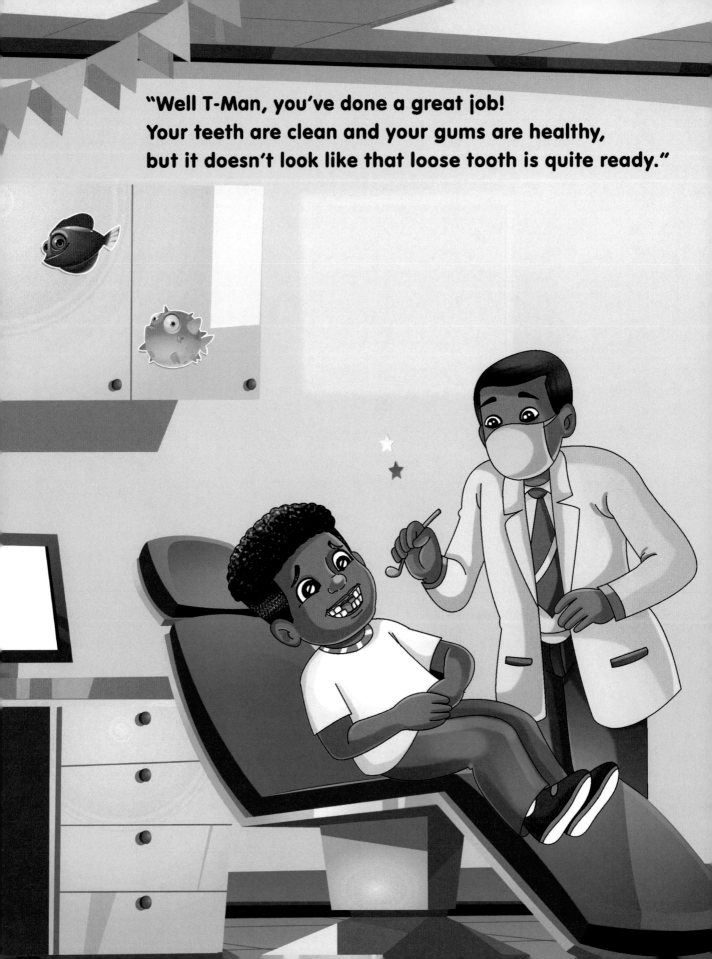

"Well T-Man, you've done a great job!
Your teeth are clean and your gums are healthy,
but it doesn't look like that loose tooth is quite ready."

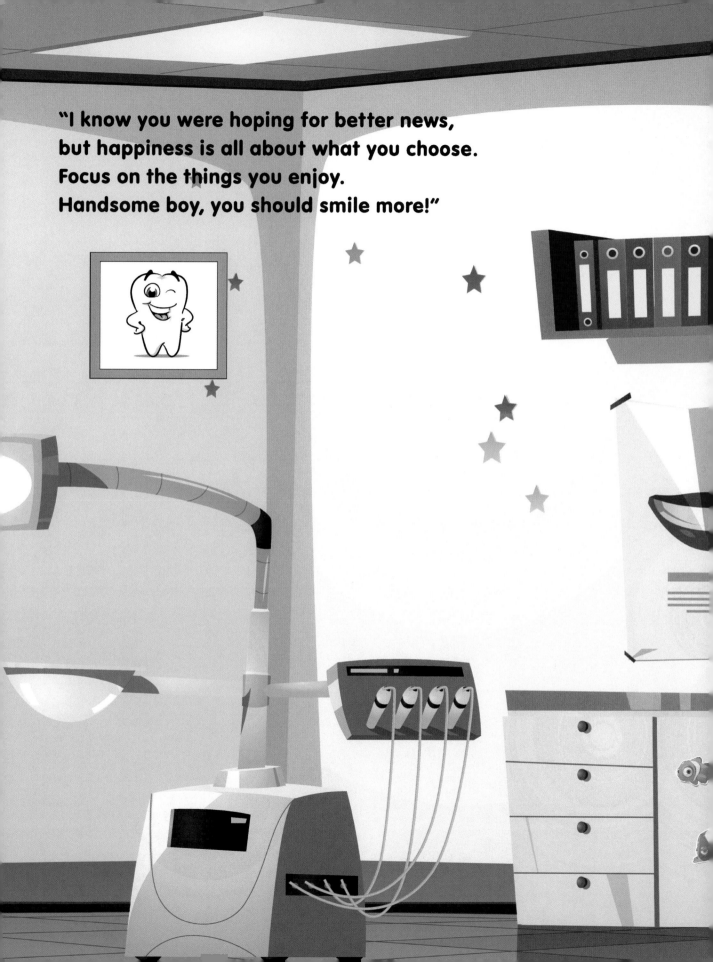

"I know you were hoping for better news,
but happiness is all about what you choose.
Focus on the things you enjoy.
Handsome boy, you should smile more!"

"Now why the long face? It'll come out with time," Trent's mom expresses with a smile as she drives.

But Trent isn't listening; he's too busy worrying about his tooth.

"I'll just ask my friends, they always know what to do. Mommy, mommy! Hurry, I need to get to school!"

Trent races to get to class.
"Sorry mom, I have to get there pretty fast."

She yells, "Son, you can't rush your whole life away!
Patience is key. Where is your smile today?

You cannot hide it forever because life is full of joy.
Handsome boy, you should smile more!"

Trent's teacher smiles as he enters the room.
"Nice of you to join us today.
Your classmates are already out to play.
Did you happen to lose your smile while you were away?"

Trent sighs,
"I just need to know what to do to make my tooth come out real soon."

"Well, you know what they say,
an apple a day keeps the dentist away.
Here, take a bite! This should do the trick.
I bet that tooth will come out quick."

Crunch, crunch! Still no luck!
"Maybe another bite will get me that extra buck!"
Crunch! Crunch! Crunch! Crunch!
"Waiting for this tooth sucks!" Trent exclaims.

"Just hang in there; it will come out some way.
Now run along, before you miss your time to play.
Do not be so down, you will turn into a bore.
Handsome boy, you should smile more."

Trent's friends greet him.
"What's up man, dentist today right?"
Did something happen?
You look so uptight."

"Well, I wanted the tooth fairy to show up tonight,
but the dentist says the timing just isn't right.
I have never had a problem. I am not sure what to do.
Do you guys have ideas because I have no clue." Trent says.

"Give it a little wiggle. Maybe a little jiggle..."
Star says as she giggles.

Candice offers candy but that doesn't come in handy.

"I've got the answer!" Malachi yells as Trent takes his last crunch. "We will get that baby out with just one punch."

"No way," says Trent. "I will pass on that offer."

Kayden says, "Let me give it a try; I've been here before."
"Just tie a string from your tooth to a door.
Then, stand in one spot and slam the door as fast as you can
and before you know it, that tooth will be in your hand."

"The tooth fairy will come. Believe me, it is true.
My dad did this with me and I lost not one, but TWO!"

Trent's friends await to see the results.
They tie the string and slam the door, but still no luck!
Kaboom! Kaboom! Let's try once more!
Kaboom! Kaboom! This time it'll work for sure!

"Now what's all this noise? You guys had better settle down, grab your belongings and get ready for dismissal," Ms. Harris frowns.

Trent whispers, "It's okay, we tried." with his head hanging low.
Then heads to his mom's car, as it is time to go.

"There is my handsome boy! Did your day turn out just fine?
Or did you focus on your tooth the whole time?
Wait, do not tell me; I can see it on your face.
Should I remind you of your affirmations for the day?"

"No thanks, I got it. Thanks for trying to help.
I will just have to remember some things for myself."

Trent whispers,
"Kings are still kings even when things don't go the way we plan.
I am handsome, I am smart. Anything I want to do, I can.
I must be patient; it will happen in time.
It gets even better when you free it from your mind."

So, he decides not to worry.

**Trent completes his homework,
eats dinner with his family,
and prepares himself for bed.
Not a thought of his tooth and not a worry in his head.**

Right before bed, he brushes his teeth.
Then all of a sudden, something falls in the sink...

Trent is excited. It has finally happened!!
He rushes off to bed to wait for the magic.

My dearest Trent,
I decided to leave you $5 this time
For your patience, strength, and wise little mind.
You have a light the world has not seen before!
Handsome boy, you should smile more!

Made in the USA
Columbia, SC
29 January 2021